MASK™

CAR WARS

Miles Mayhem, the ruthless leader of the evil organisation VENOM, was in a jolly mood. "Contraworld scientists have just delivered a new device to me that they feel can help us to destroy MASK forever," he explained to Dagger and Rax.

"Why would Contraworld send us a souped-up armband?" Dagger asked, as Mayhem fitted the strange device to his arm.

"Because," Mayhem replied, "this so called 'armband' is going to be the key to the defeat of MASK."

Mayhem held his arm with the device on up in the air. "This box of electronic tricks will allow me to control all the MASK vehicles whenever they come in range," he laughed. As the possibilities of what Mayhem was saying became apparent, the evil spies also joined in the mocking laughter.

The next day, Matt was called to MASK control in Boulder Hill to hear some bad news from Duane, the head of Spectrum. "Sorry to call you out, Matt," the Spectrum leader and Matt's friend said, "but we have just learnt that VENOM are making an attack on the Atlantic Tunnel."

Recently work had been finished on the 3,000 mile long tunnel under the Atlantic ocean joining America and Europe together. Now it looked like VENOM was about to break that vital connection.

"We're on our way," Matt responded. Soon after that the Rhino, Condor and Gator were speeding along the highway to the Atlantic Tunnel.

Inside the three high-tech vehicles sat four of the bravest men alive. Matt Trakker and Bruce Sato drove the incredibly powerful Rhino truck. Next to them on the road was the open-topped Gator with the devil-may-care driver, Buddie Hawks. Flying above them, to scout ahead, was the Condor, a motorcycle which could, like now, become a mini-helicopter, piloted by Brad Turner.

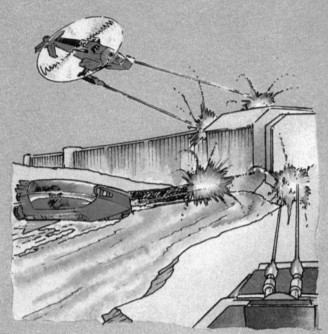

As MASK raced to the scene of the VENOM attack, Mayhem had already put his master plan into operation. "MASK will soon be here," Mayhem told himself as he casually fired his laser at the tunnel below, "and when they arrive I will destroy them."

"Battle stations!" ordered Matt as the MASK team came across the VENOM attack.

"Let's get 'em," encouraged Turner as he thundered forward in the Condor, his lasers cutting into the side of Mayhem's Switchblade.

"They think they are so smart," Mayhem told himself, "but this will wipe those smirks from their faces." As Mayhem finished he pressed the switch on his new weapon. Immediately a red light flashed on to tell him it had been activated.

Mayhem's evil laughter sounded like a machine gun as he watched the trio of MASK vehicles tumble out of control.

Taken by surprise, Buddie Hawks was knocked from his seat and he crashed onto the open roadway as his Gator sped away from him.

With Hawks helpless on the roadway, Mayhem seized his chance. He pressed the controls and smiled as he watched the Gator turn around and speed towards Hawks. "You can be the first to go," Mayhem said, "but you will not be the last."

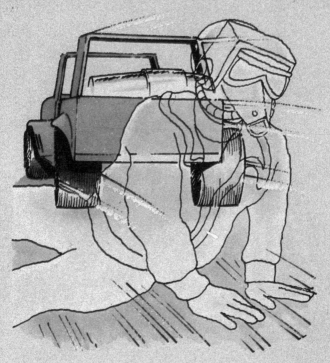

Hawks moved with lightning action and energised his Penetrator Mask to allow the Gator to pass harmlessly through his body. He felt a cold shiver as the Gator passed through his ghostly form.

As Hawks made his escape from the Gator, his friends were all being thrown from their vehicles. As Sato hit the soft, sandy ground, his eyes caught a movement in the sky. It was Turner, knocked from his battle-bike and falling to certain doom!

"Lifter, on!" responded Sato.

From his MASK visor a beam of particles engulfed the falling Turner and lowered him safely to the ground. Within moments the four MASK agents were standing together, their masks primed for action.

"What's going on?" Turner asked as he regained his breath.

"Somehow Mayhem has taken control of the MASK machines," Matt answered.

Before he could say anything more he was interrupted by Hawks. "Heads up, guys . . . we have company!" he shouted as the Condor swooped towards them with its lasers slicing through the air.

"The tunnel . . ." indicated Sato as he began to run towards the opening leading from the ocean.

"He's right," continued Matt, "once inside we'll have some cover."

Immediately the foursome ran towards the metal tunnel.

As the MASK agents dashed towards
the protection of the tunnel they heard
the mounting sound of the Rhino and
Gator engines as they began to charge
towards them. With mere seconds to
spare, the MASK agents made it into
the tunnel, the sound of laser fire close
behind them.

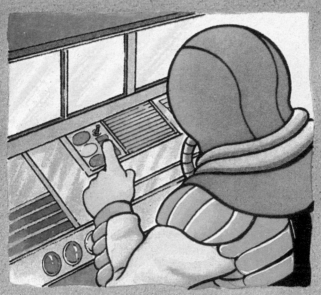

Just inside the main doors was the large control room. "Just what we need," exclaimed Sato as he ran into the computer-lined room. Within moments he was programming the computer to close the doors to the tunnel. His work was answered with a whirling sound as the mighty doors closed behind the MASK agents.

"They have used super-heavy doors
on this tunnel, in case of floods,"
explained Sato, "it will take forever for
VENOM to break in."

"Yeah, but we are also trapped,"
observed Turner as he looked around
at the massive control complex.

"Well, that's not strictly true," Hawks said from the back of the room, "I still have my Penetrator Mask."

"Of course," Matt interrupted, "your mask allows you to pass through solid objects."

"Which means I can pay Miles Mayhem a little surprise call and learn what's going on," continued Hawks as he walked towards a solid wall.

"See you guys later." Hawks cheerfully waved as he walked through the metre thick wall. As he emerged on the outside he found himself almost next to Mayhem's Switchblade. "Old nasty must've landed to plan his next move," Hawks decided as he moved closer to the blue VENOM plane.

"This device allows me to control all the MASK vehicles," Mayhem was saying into his microphone, unaware that MASK eyes were watching him. "They can't stay inside forever, and when they come out we'll be waiting for them."

Having heard everything he needed to hear, Hawks began to make his way back to the tunnel.

Once back inside the tunnel, Hawks explained what he had seen and heard. "Any chance that you can build something to stop Mayhem?" Matt asked Sato.

"I should be able to build a 'jammer' to 'jam' – or stop – his signals to our machines," Sato answered.

"Go to it," Matt ordered.

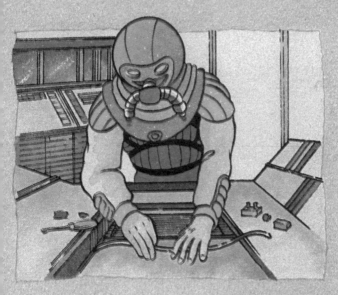

In the control room, Sato began to strip all the electrical and electronic equipment that they didn't need. Then, using the security transmitter he began to build his jammer. "It's a good job this tunnel is not in public use yet," Turner commented as they waited. "Could you imagine this place packed with trucks and autos?"

As one of the greatest electronic designers in the world, it didn't take Sato too long to rig up the device. "Here it is," he said proudly as he showed it to his fellow agents.

"Well, let's give it a try," suggested Matt, giving the signal to open the tunnel doors. "Once outside run for our vehicles," he called as the team ran towards the opening doors.

"What madness," exclaimed Mayhem as he saw the MASK agents running out of the tunnel. "They must have decided to go down in a blaze of glory," he decided, pressing the control button on his armband. "I'll destroy them with their own vehicles," he concluded.

"Impossible!" Mayhem screamed as the agents made it to the MASK machines. "Somehow they have jammed my signal . . . well, in that case I'll have to destroy them in the old fashioned way. ATTACK!" he ordered. Within seconds the VENOM vehicles were charging towards MASK.

What had been a peaceful beachline mere seconds ago, erupted into a battlefield of incredible noise and firepower. Having lost the chance of surprise so vital to VENOM winning the fight, Mayhem decided to be devious. Lowering the Switchblade above the important flood locks on the tunnel, he fired his Stinger missile at the easy to hit spot.

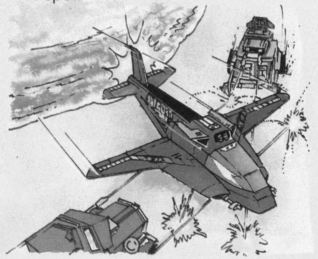

Moments later a massive explosion ripped the side of the tunnel. Almost immediately water began to flow into the gap that had just been created by Mayhem's rocket.

"The tunnel!" called Matt. "We must save the tunnel . . . even if it means that Mayhem escapes."

"Just as I planned," commented Mayhem as he pulled his copter into jet-mode and blasted away from the disaster scene. "Pull out," he radioed to his agents. Through his vid-screen he could see Rax and Dagger speeding away to safety below.

"Hawks! The Gator . . ." called Matt to the MASK agent.

"Way ahead of you," replied Hawks as he released the Gator hydroplane into the ocean. "I'll stop the water if you can plug the hole," he promised.

"Deal!" answered Matt.

Once in the water, Hawks sped towards the hole in the tunnel and set the hydroplane into whirlpool mode. The plane began to spin at an incredible speed, creating a 'hole' in the water, one of the 'sides' of which was next to the hole in the tunnel. Immediately the water stopped pouring through the gap into the open passageway.

Once the hole was cleared, Sato made his move. He energised his mask and began to lift large amounts of sand into the air. Carrying it over to the hole, he cut the beam and allowed the sand to fall into the gap. Within three trips the hole was plugged.

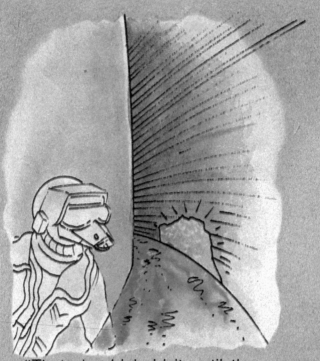

"That should hold it until the rescue services arrive," guessed Sato as he dropped the last of the sand into place.

"I'll make sure everything's alright inside," Hawks said as he used his mask to walk through the tunnel wall.

Two minutes later, Hawks reported that everything was safe inside.

"Good, I've radioed the services from the Rhino," Matt said as he began to check the MASK machines.

"That was close," Sato commented, now that all the vehicles had been checked.

"Yes. VENOM are getting more dangerous," Matt replied.

As MASK drove back to Boulder Hill, Matt couldn't help but think about how VENOM had been stopped that day. Each agent had worked together. Each had risked everything to help MASK and his fellow agents. Suddenly Matt didn't feel as worried about VENOM.

Sato was sitting beside Matt in the Rhino. "What are you thinking, Matt?" the brave agent asked.

"Oh, about VENOM," Matt confessed. "I was just a bit worried that they were getting more powerful with the backing of Contraworld. Then I realised that we have a weapon they can never have."

"What's that, old friend?" asked Sato.

"Exactly that," replied Matt with a smile. "We have friendship and loyalty. Which means we work as a team. And that will also defeat the likes of VENOM."

"Amen to that," said Turner and Hawks, who had heard the conversation over the MASK radios.

Suddenly, the day felt a lot better.